Surprise!
It's Just Pee

La Manda Davis

Trilogy Christian Publishers
A Wholly Owned Subsidary of Trinity Broadcasting Network
2442 Michelle Drive
Tustin, CA 92780

For information, address Trilogy Christian Publishing
Rights Department, 2442 Michelle Drive, Tustin, Ca 92780.
Trilogy Christian Publishing/ TBN and colophon are trademarks of Trinity Broadcasting Network.

For information about special discounts for bulk purchases, please contact Trilogy Christian Publishing.

Manufactured in the United States of America

10 9 8 7 6 5 4 3 2 1

Library of Congress Cataloging-in-Publication Data is available.

ISBN 978-1-64773-222-6 (Print Book)
ISBN 978-1-64773-223-3 (ebook)

For all girls 'around the world' especially, Gianna Floyd and Laurenna Plourd... OUR dreams and voices...Matter (Jeremiah 29:11).

When Tangerine plays, she's happy, she's fast, she's classy, and a bit sassy. Don't put her in her cage,

or you will come home from school to find your homework super wet and sappy. Surprise! It's just pee.

Tangerine loves to take baths!
Splish, splash, plop, thump!

5

However, if she's scared, blue, or she just misses you, surprise! It's just pee—on your bed.

Tangerine loves to visit Grandma Tee Tee! Grandma Tee Tee and Tangerine play together all the time! Grandma Tee Tee's house is filled with fun, food, and love.

Tangerine has so much fun that she gets sleepy and lays in the sun. So sleepy that Tangerine sleeps in Grandma Tee Tee's bed all night long!

Snore, snooze. Purrrr.

Uh oh! Tangerine must have had one of her adventurous dreams! Oops! Surprise! It's just pee—in Grandma Tee Tee's bed.

15

One day, Grandma Tee Tee asks Tangerine, "Tangerine, why do you not pee in your potty box?" Tangerine raises her head and gracefully says, "Mandy and I are going shopping today to select a special, small box made just for me!" Grandma Tee Tee smiles.

Today is the day! Today is the day that Tangerine will find her special box. Mandy walks Tangerine in Tangerine's boo boo cart to PetMart Plus—a boutique store for those fun and sophisticated kinds of pets! The aisle is long, large, and brightly colorful, with active cats on the potty box, modeled as superstars. Some boxes are scented, some boxes are not. Then, finally, Tangerine sees it. The potty box made just for *her, and* with her favorite colors!

17

Sitting
Pretty

19

When Tangerine and Mandy arrive home, Mandy opens Tangerine's potty box and sprinkles the small purple beads, scented with lavender and vanilla. Tangerine gets so excited, she wants to pee in *her* special box. It will be hers!

21

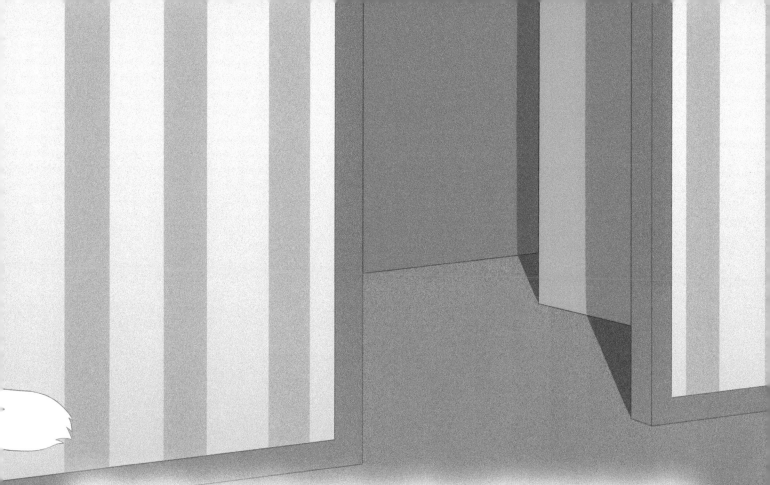

When it's quiet, Tangerine walks confidently down the hallway into Mandy's bathroom and steps into her box. Tangerine scratches the lavender-vanilla scented beads and...

When Grandma Tee Tee hears the great news, Grandma Tee Tee smiles and hugs Tangerine out of love. She thinks to herself, "This is the beginning of a journey."

Surprise! It's just The End.

CPSIA information can be obtained
at www.ICGtesting.com
Printed in the USA
LVHW070529040920
664825LV00006B/263

9 781647 732226